the ANT BULLY™

THE GREAT ANT ADVENTURE

ADAPTED BY QUINLAN B. LEE
BASED ON THE SCREENPLAY BY JOHN A. DAVIS

SCHOLASTIC INC.

New York   Toronto   London   Auckland   Sydney

Mexico City   New Delhi   Hong Kong   Buenos Aires

JP
Lee

First published in the UK by Scholastic Ltd, 2006
Scholastic Children's Books, Euston House, 24 Eversholt Street, London NW1 1DB, UK

ISBN 0-439-85680-9

12 11 10 9 8 7 6 5 4 3 2   6 7 8 9 10/0

Printed in the U.S.A.
First printing, July 2006

Lucas Nicklc was a
bully. He liked to pick
on the ants that lived
in his front yard.

Inside the colony, the ants called Lucas "The Destroyer." They lived in constant fear of him. They panicked each time his footsteps shook the mound.

Finally, the ants had had enough. Late one night, the ant wizard Zoc snuck into Lucas's room. He put a tiny drop of magic potion into Lucas's ear and Lucas shrank down to the size of an ant!

Back at the colony, the Queen decided Lucas needed to be taught a lesson.

"You must become an ant!" she announced.

Luckily, a kind ant named Hova volunteered to help Lucas find his place in the colony.

With the help of her friends, Fugax and Kreela, Hova taught Lucas the basics of ant life—scouting, foraging, and surviving.

One day, Lucas's new friends showed him a cave painting of a creature they called "The Cloud Breather."

Oh, no! Lucas thought to himself. *That's an exterminator!*

Suddenly, Lucas remembered that he had just signed a contract with the exterminator. He and the ants were in serious trouble! He had to figure out a way to cancel that contract.

Then, Lucas had an idea.

"The colony needs food, right?" he asked his friends. "Well, my house is filled with food."

Lucas figured once he was inside the house, he could call the exterminator to cancel the contract.

But he forgot that being the size of an ant made things more difficult.

"Oh, man," said Lucas. "Why did Mom have to get shag carpet?! It'll take days to get to the kitchen. Unless . . ."

Lucas saw his mom's rose petals caught in the blast of air from the fan. Seeing them float across the room gave him an idea.

"Come on!" Lucas called. "Let's go hang gliding!"

Hova looked down at the whirring fan. "Have you ever done this before?" she asked.

"No, but I played the video game," Lucas replied. "Come on, everyone. Follow meeeeeeeeeeeee!"

Lucas jumped over the edge with Hova, Kreela, and Fugax not far behind him.

The four friends plummeted toward the fan blades, until *WHOOSH!* A blast of air launched them upward again. Soon they were zooming around the Nickles' living room.

"Awesome!" Lucas yelled.
"Yahooooo!" screamed Fugax.
"Show-off!" Kreela called after them.

The ants were amazed by the Nickles' house. "It must have taken thousands of humans to build this," Hova marveled.

As they sailed past a painting of Hawaii, Lucas told them all about his family's vacation there. "It's got volcanoes, hula dancers, Don Ho, and surfboards. I even caught a fish!"

Finally, they made it to the kitchen.

Fugax spied the sweet rocks first. "Woo hoo!" he cheered. "It's the mother lode!"

"Let's start gathering," said Kreela.

Lucas spotted the exterminator's card on the fridge. He quickly memorized the phone number and then dashed to the phone.

Lucas dialed the number by jumping on the huge number pad.

"This is Lucas Nickle!" he shouted into the phone. "I want to cancel my order. NO EXTERMINATOR!"

Suddenly, they heard a door slam.
"What was that?" Hova asked.
Lucas froze. "Oh, no! Tiffany!"

His sister was home, and the first thing she always came looking for was the phone!

"What's a Tiffany?" Hova wondered.

"You don't want to know," Lucas replied. "Run!"

They raced to the kitchen sink and jumped down the drain to freedom.

"Lucas, you saved us," Hova said.

"*And* we got lots of sweet rocks!" Fugax cheered. "Unbelievable!"

Lucas beamed at his friends.

By helping his friends escape from Tiffany, Lucas had proven that he could be an ant. The Queen declared that Lucas could finally go home to his family.

Lucas realized everything really is bigger when you're small, even your adventures.